Living Lights™
A Faith Story

The Berenstain Bea[rs]

Hugs and Kisses

Sticker & Activity Book

Jan & Mike Berenstain

Requests for information should be addressed to:
Zonderkidz, 3900 Sparks Drive SE, Grand Rapids, Michigan 49546

ISBN 978-0-310-75382-7

Zonderkidz is trademark of Zondervan.

Editor: Mary Hassinger
Interior design: Kris Nelson
Cover design: Diane Mielke

Printed in China

22 23 24 25 26 27 28 /DSC/ 7 6 5 4 3

Lots of Love Matching

Families have lots of love to share. Match the mother or father with the baby. Draw a line.

Friends are the Best

Where is Cousin Fred? Brother cannot find his friend.
Help him through the maze.

START

END

A Great Time Together

The Bear family is going on a picnic. Gran and Gramps are coming too. Color the picture. Add stickers to help finish the picture. Draw some animal friends too.

Love One Another

Use the code below to find out what the Bible says about love.

A	=	1	J	=	10	S	=	19
B	=	2	K	=	11	T	=	20
C	=	3	L	=	12	U	=	21
D	=	4	M	=	13	V	=	22
E	=	5	N	=	14	W	=	23
F	=	6	O	=	15	X	=	24
G	=	7	P	=	16	Y	=	25
H	=	8	Q	=	17	Z	=	26
I	=	9	R	=	18			

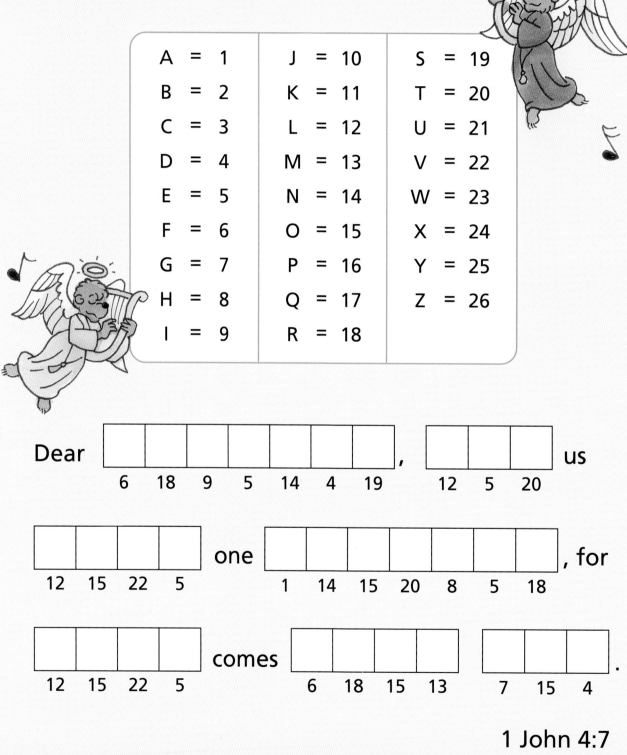

Dear ☐☐☐☐☐☐☐ , ☐☐☐ us
6 18 9 5 14 4 19   12 5 20

☐☐☐☐ one ☐☐☐☐☐☐☐ , for
12 15 22 5   1 14 15 20 8 5 18

☐☐☐☐ comes ☐☐☐☐ ☐☐☐ .
12 15 22 5   6 18 15 13   7 15 4

1 John 4:7

Dear friends, let us love one another, for love comes from God.

6

1-2-3, Color Me

"Let's take a walk today," says Grizzly Gramps. "I love spending time with my grandbears." Color the picture. Use the key below.

1 = green   5 = blue
2 = brown   6 = light brown
3 = pink   7 = yellow
4 = red   8 = light blue

Bear Family Fun

The Bear family may be a busy family but they always find time to spend together. Help the Bears find 8 hidden things. Circle them.

Connect It

Friends can be young, old, big, small, near, or far. Connect the dots to meet one of the Bear family's good friends—Farmer Ben! Then color the picture of these friends.

Hugs and Kisses Word Search

Find and circle words about love. Use the Word Bank.

```
P Y F L Z D K W O Y N F R S J F O R R T
W D J A P I H S D N E I R F P O J Y N H
A P U X T E L O V E O E Y R K I L Z I K
X V H D H H E F X M W O V Z M T M I T Q
U L T C J G E D Q O K I S S E S R V O G
O O E C D P W R L T Z P U Y G O S A X I
F X N T F C U F Y H F E U V I G P J E D
S U S E J T O W Q E K T M S U N T T G H
C W W Q Z E N Y J R L S I H B F G R D D
P R J Y U I W D G S I I P Y D T M D K W
S A J J R S I N G S Q B K K E O M U J N
I D J H I O M A I E E L V E P H E O Z L
Y W C S S R B C I W Y J G K U S Y U E R
Z P T H W R V H W H U Q T S M Z A K H E
W E S A K E F E G T Y U K V P J I J H N
R M G U X H T O A I Y P F P X D P R E Y
M H X L G T N U H K E G F G D D K G M O
I M H B E O Z W E Q O N O B E O V U R G
I S D L I R C V B R Z R E L J S N G Q A
R V B T B B N U J V J A N F H I L Y O I
```

WORD BANK

- BROTHER
- CANDY
- FATHER
- FLOWERS
- FRIENDSHIP
- HEART
- HUGS
- JESUS
- JOY
- KISSES
- LIKE
- LOVE
- MOTHER
- NEIGHBOR
- PETS
- SISTER

It's Gone!

Oh, no! How many are left? Solve by subtraction. Circle the correct number.

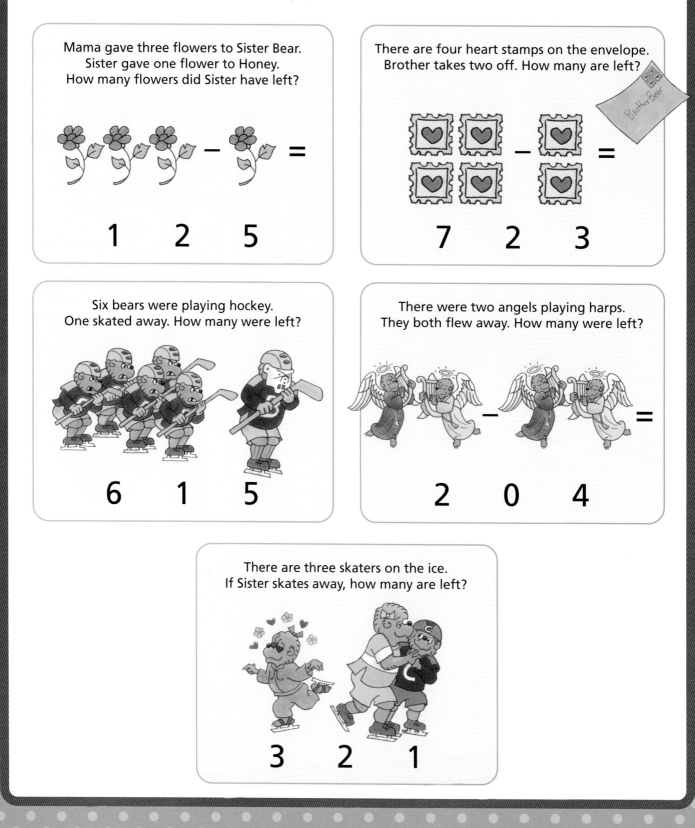

Mama gave three flowers to Sister Bear.
Sister gave one flower to Honey.
How many flowers did Sister have left?

1   2   5

There are four heart stamps on the envelope.
Brother takes two off. How many are left?

7   2   3

Six bears were playing hockey.
One skated away. How many were left?

6   1   5

There were two angels playing harps.
They both flew away. How many were left?

2   0   4

There are three skaters on the ice.
If Sister skates away, how many are left?

3   2   1

What's the Difference?

Sister and Lizzy are best friends. They love doing things together, like picking flowers. Look at these pictures of Lizzy and Sister. There are 6 differences. Circle them.

Animal Friends

The Bear family has lots of animal friends. They live around the tree house on the sunny dirt road. Read and follow the directions. Stick the stickers. See all the animals that come to see the Bears every day!

1. Put two red birds in the sky to the right of the tree house.

2. Put a turtle in the road by the Bear's mailbox.

3. Put two hopping bunnies by the fence.

4. Help a bluebird sit on top of the round window in the tree house.

5. Deer like apples. Put four deer by the apple trees.

6. Look at the duck family by Papa's workshop.

God's Creation

God shows us his great love through creation. Color this picture of God's creation. Use stickers to help you finish the picture.

Big, Bigger, Biggest

Look at the rows of pictures that show friends in Bear Country. Which is biggest in each row? Find the sticker that matches and cover the biggest friend in each row.

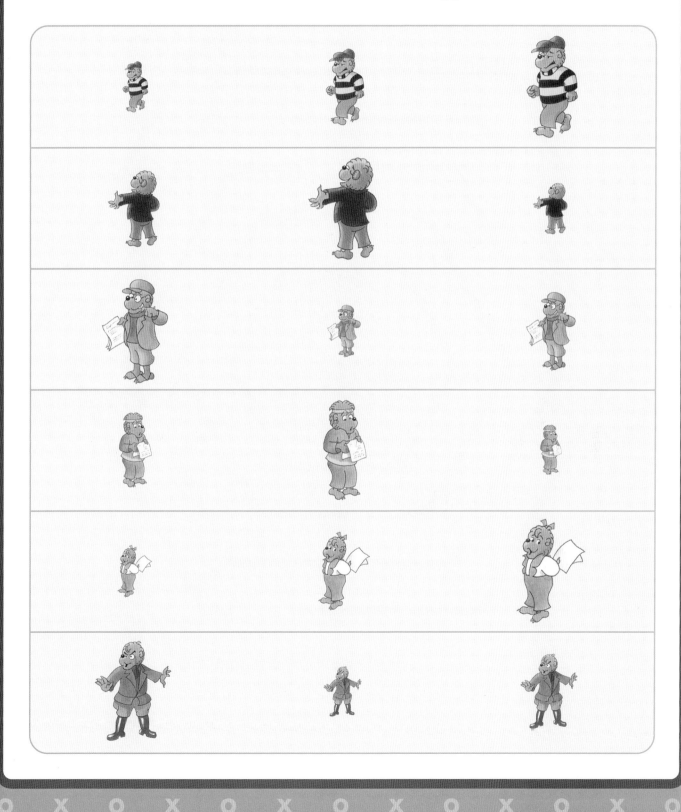

Where is Mama Bear?

Papa Bear is looking for Mama. He has flowers for her.
Help Papa find Mama.

START

Which Is It?

Three of these Bear Country friends are the same. One is different.
Circle the one that is different.

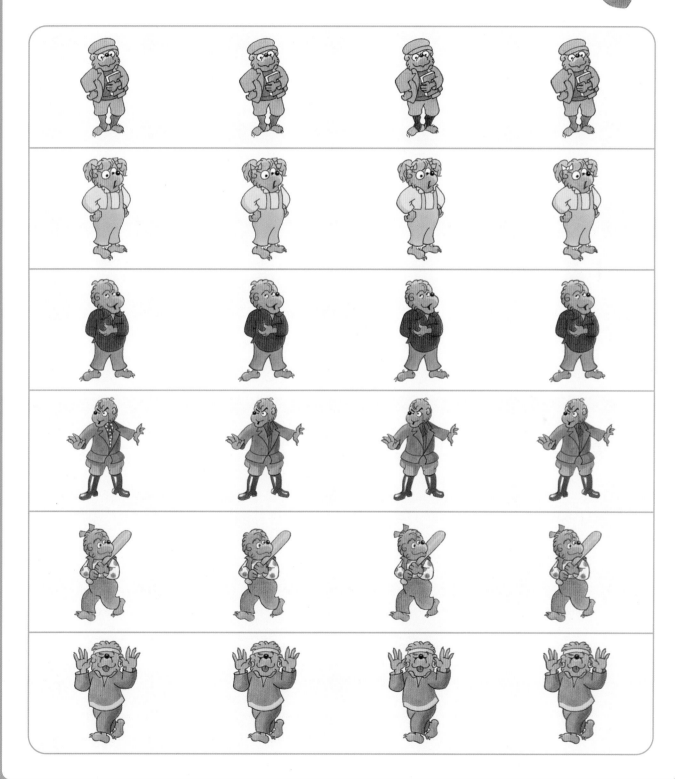

Brother and Sister Time

It's fun to spend time with a brother or sister. Being outside is special too. Find the ten hidden hearts. Cover them with the red heart stickers.

We Love Word Searches

Find the words in the word search. Circle the words. Use the Word Bank.

```
            R  G  I  A                    B  C  M  U
            V  Y  Z  L  Z  D           T  A  E  P  Z  I
         P  Q  D  R  L  X  G  A     T  W  D  V  V  H  C  Z
         R  R  E  P  M  B  T  B  O  D  J  H  E  F  G  X  U  X  U  K
      C  E  O  Z  T  J  S  R  T  N  L  F  E  T  C  Z  C  H  L  O  V  E
   J  Y  T  P  D  K  S  Z  D  Q  O  O  R  V  C  X  U  L  C  F  H  H  L  U
   K  H  H  H  K  Q  D  X  A  F  A  M  I  L  Y  N  T  V  E  A  J  L  F  Z
   Z  D  G  W  W  A  I  K  Q  B  U  M  E  F  J  T  G  W  P  E  J  I  R  O
   U  X  U  P  H  Y  L  Z  H  W  A  D  N  F  T  U  C  P  L  G  E  W  S  B
   S  N  A  F  M  S  D  A  A  P  K  X  D  I  Y  R  Y  K  T  I  Z  S  U  K
   I  A  L  K  I  S  S  D  E  E  S  B  S  I  S  H  S  N  F  I  L  V  D  A
   S  Q  K  T  Y  O  C  O  D  X  J  P  Q  S  H  P  N  O  P  B  R  F
   H  X  G  B  C  E  R  D  K  B  N  K  Q  T  X  C  S  T  G  X  E  Y
   U  S  N  W  L  I  I  D  X  S  O  D  L  X  F  T  O  H  B  M
      T  Z  N  L  Y  P  I  O  O  J  W  P  M  M  Q  E  Q  I
      C  G  S  H  U  G  E  N  I  T  N  E  L  A  V  F
      H  Z  M  C  A  N  D  Y  S  Y  N  X  Q  X
      E  J  I  I  N  G  E  F  B  Y  Y  U
      N  A  L  E  B  P  F  D  F  B
      N  L  E  I  J  W  B  H
      L  F  A  S  X  M
      C  M  E  F
      M  D
```

WORD BANK

- ☐ LOVE
- ☐ HUG
- ☐ KISS
- ☐ HAPPY
- ☐ CUPID
- ☐ VALENTINE
- ☐ LAUGHTER
- ☐ FRIENDS
- ☐ SMILE
- ☐ CANDY
- ☐ FAMILY
- ☐ PETS

Love is GREAT

Use the code below to find out what the Bible says about love.

A = 1	G = 7	M = 13	S = 19	W = 23
B = 2	H = 8	N = 14	T = 20	X = 24
C = 3	I = 9	O = 15	U = 21	Y = 25
D = 4	J = 10	P = 16	V = 22	Z = 26
E = 5	K = 11	Q = 17		
F = 6	L = 12	R = 18		

And now ☐☐☐☐☐ ☐☐☐☐☐
20 8 5 19 5   20 8 18 5 5

☐☐☐☐☐☐ : ☐☐☐☐☐ ,
18 5 13 1 9 14   6 1 9 20 8

☐☐☐☐ and ☐☐☐☐ . But the
8 15 16 5   12 15 22 5

☐☐☐☐☐☐☐☐ of these
7 18 5 1 20 5 19 20

☐☐ ☐☐☐☐ .
9 19   12 15 22 5

1 Corinthians 13:13

And now these three remain: faith, hope and love. But the greatest of these is love. 1 Corinthians 13:13

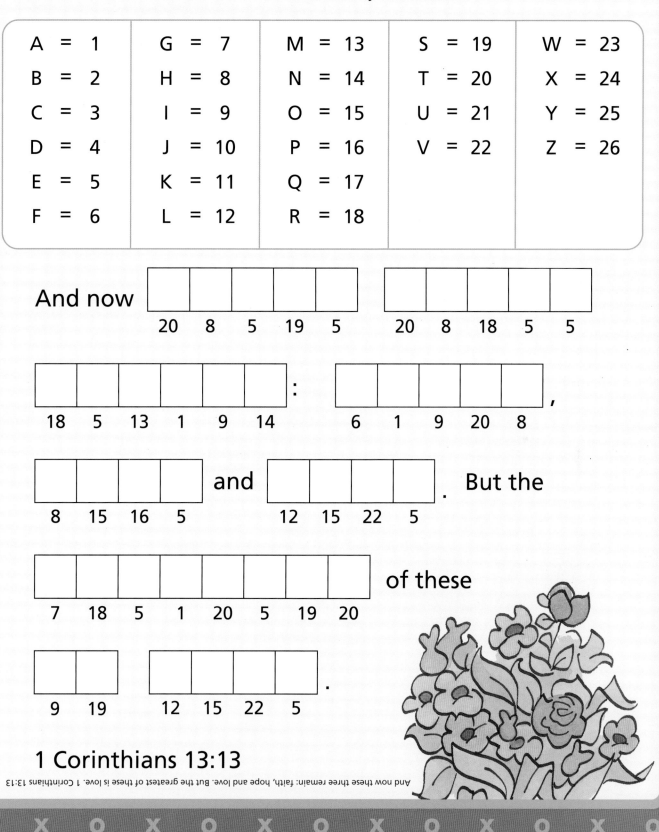

23

Good Neighbor Bears

You can show love in many ways. One way is to be a good neighbor. The Bear family says hello to their neighbors as they all walk to Chapel in the Woods.

Color the picture. Use stickers to help finish.

It's Good to Make New Friends

Look at the picture. There is a new friend visiting the Bear family! Good friends belong. But there are 8 things that do not belong in this picture. Circle them.

Color It with Love

The Bear family is walking to Chapel in the Woods. They will hear Preacher Brown talk about God's love. Color this picture of God's creation in Bear Country.

God Shows His Love

Noah and his family loved God. God loved Noah. He showed Noah how much he loved him by sending a rainbow when the rain stopped. Read about Noah in Genesis 6. Look at the picture. Finish it with stickers.

Do You Love the Berenstain Bears?

Fill in the blanks. Use the Word Bank. Then find a sticker for the box after each.

_____ Bear is the oldest cub in the Bear family. He likes to play hockey.

_____ grows many good things the Bear family and their friends and neighbors eat.

The baby cub's name is _____ Bear. She loves Mama and Papa very much.

The Mama, Papa, and the cubs love to spend time with Grizzly _____ and _____.

The Bear family lives in a _____.

_____ Bear always wears a pink bow in her hair.

Cousin _____ is one of Brother's good friends.

The Bear family goes to _____ _____ to hear about God's love.

WORD BANK

❑ Honey
❑ Brother
❑ Sister

❑ Gran
❑ Gramps
❑ Chapel in the Woods

❑ Farmer Ben
❑ Fred
❑ Tree house

Friend Time = Best Time

The cubs are having so much fun! But look closely. There are 6 differences in the pictures. Circle the differences.